BIG TIME BEARS

TICK TOCK

by **Stephen Krensky**
illustrated by **Maryann Cocca-Leffler**

Little, Brown and Company
Boston Toronto London

For Peter

S. K.

**To Andrew John, Evan, Andrew Ross,
and Gregory**

M. C. L.

K TOCK TICK TOCK TICK T

Text copyright © 1989 by Stephen Krensky
Illustrations copyright © 1989 by Maryann Cocca-Leffler

First edition

Library of Congress Cataloging-in-Publication Data

Krensky, Stephen.
  Big time bears/by Stephen Krensky;
illustrated by Maryann Cocca-Leffler.
     p.   cm.
  Summary: The daily activities of a bear family demonstrate the
meaning of such units of time as a second, minute, and week.
  ISBN 0-316-50375-4
  1. Time — Juvenile literature. 2. Bears — Juvenile literature.
[1. Time. 2. Bears.] I. Cocca-Leffler, Maryann, 1958–   ill.
II. Title.
QB209.5.K74 1989
529 — dc19   88-30793
                                                       CIP
                                                       AC

10 9 8 7 6 5 4 3 2 1
BP

Published simultaneously in Canada
by Little, Brown & Company (Canada) Limited

Printed in the United States of America

The Bear family takes time to do everything.
Some things take a long time,
some things take a short time,
and some things take almost no time at all.

A second is a very short amount of time.
In one second . . .

Barney Bear's alarm clock rings.

RRRING

Sarah Bear yawns.

Father Bear touches his toes.
Mother Bear pulls up the window shade.

Baby Bear squirts out
too much toothpaste.

Sixty seconds make a minute.
In one minute . . .

Sarah Bear ties her shoes.
Baby Bear puts on her boots and coat.

Father Bear gets soaked in the rain.

In one minute . . .

Father Bear parks the car.
The traffic light stays red.
A workman climbs his ladder.

Sixty minutes make an hour.
In one hour . . .

Sarah Bear picks out the perfect present.

Father and Barney Bear try on some new clothes.

In one hour . . .

Barney and his friends celebrate his birthday.

Twenty-four hours make a day.
In one day . . .

The sun comes up

and goes down

and comes up again!

In one day . . .

The Bears eat breakfast,

lunch,

and dinner.

Seven days make a week.
In one week . . .

Every day passes once.

In one week . . .

The Bears order plane tickets by phone

and receive them in the mail.

In one week . . .

The Bears take a vacation.

While back at home . . .

Newspapers and mail pile up.
The plants need watering.
The sidewalk needs shoveling.

Four weeks (plus some extra days) make a month.
In one month . . .

The moon goes around the earth.

In one month . . .

Carpenters build a new room on the house.

Twelve months make a year.
In one year . . .

The Earth goes around the sun.

In one year . . .

The young Bears go through
a whole grade at school

and have summer vacation, too!

In one year . . . the four seasons pass.

Fall

Winter

Spring

Summer

Ten years make a decade.
In one decade . . .

The house needs repainting.
Everybody gets older.

Ten decades make a century.
In one century . . .

Many things grow and change.

Including the Bear family!